D1023132

WITHDRAWN

STONE ARCH BOOKS
a capstone imprint

UP NEXT >>>

on Sports Illustrated KIDS

:02 **SPORTS ZONE SPECIAL REPORT**

:04 **FEATURE PRESENTATION:**

HOOP RAT

FOLLOWED BY:

:50 **SPORTS ZONE POSTGAME RECAP**

:51 **SPORTS ZONE POSTGAME EXTRA**

:52 **SI KIDS INFO CENTER**

FORMER GOLIATHS TEAM CAPTAIN JOINS SPARTANS SQUAD **SIK TICKER**

TEAMMATES NERVOUS ABOUT NEWEST SPARTAN

TREY McTIERNAN

STATS:
AGE: 14
POSITION: GUARD

BIO: Trey McTiernan and Max Kendricks will definitely send the already surging Spartans right into the playoffs — that is, if they can learn to trust their new teammate, Griffin Henshaw. Trey isn't convinced that Griff's loyalty lies with the Spartans — he is the former team captain of the Goliaths, who just so happen to be the Spartans' biggest rivals. Trey's facing some tough choices in the coming season...

GRIFFIN HENSHAW

AGE: 14

POSITION: GUARD

BIO: Griffin wasn't happy that his family had to move — his teammates on the Goliaths are also his best friends, so leaving them was doubly painful for the talented teen. He was also the Goliaths' team captain, which has more than a few of his new teammates nervous about him joining their squad.

COACH SCHUSTER

AGE: 47

BIO: Coach "Schu" used to play bass guitar for a well-known rock band. He loves basketball just as much as music.

COACH SCHU

MAX KENDRICKS

AGE: 14   **POSITION:** FORWARD

BIO: Max thinks that trust is earned, not given — and that Griffin will have to work hard to gain the Spartans' loyalty.

KENDRICKS

BONK!

PRESENTS

HOOP RAT

A PRODUCTION OF

▼ STONE ARCH BOOKS
a capstone imprint

written by *Scott Ciencin*
illustrated by *Aburtov*
penciled by *Fernando Cano*
inked by *Andres Esparza*
colored by *Fares Maese*

designed and directed by *Bob Lentz*
edited by *Sean Tulien*
creative direction by *Heather Kindseth*
editorial management by *Donald Lemke*
editorial direction by *Michael Dahl*

Summary: Trey, the Spartans' team captain, becomes fast friends with Griffin, the newest member of their squad. The problem is, Griff used to play for the Spartans' biggest rivals, the Goliaths, and the rest of the Spartans think he's a rat. Trey doesn't know what to do. His teammates want him to betray his friendship with Griff to save their season . . . but if they're wrong about Griff, then Trey will end up being the rat.

Sports Illustrated KIDS *Hoop Rat* is published by Stone Arch Books,
1710 Roe Crest Drive, North Mankato, Minnesota 56003.
www.capstonepub.com

Copyright © 2011 by Stone Arch Books, a Capstone imprint.

All rights reserved. No part of this publication may be reproduced in whole or in part, or stored in a retrieval system, or transmitted in any form or by any means, electronic, mechanical, photocopying, recording, or otherwise, without written permission of the publisher, or where applicable Time Inc.
For information regarding permissions, write to Stone Arch Books,
1710 Roe Crest Drive, North Mankato, Minnesota 56003.
SI KIDS is a trademark of Time Inc. Used with permission.

Printed in the United States of America in Stevens Point, Wisconsin.
122014   008660R

Library of Congress Cataloging-in-Publication Data
Ciencin, Scott.
  Hoop rat / written by Scott Ciencin ; illustrated by Aburtov, Cano, Fernando, Esparza, Andres and Fares Maese.
    p. cm. -- (Sports Illustrated kids graphic novels)
  ISBN 978-1-4342-2223-7 (library binding)
  ISBN 978-1-4342-3069-0 (paperback)
  ISBN 978-1-4342-4947-0 (e-book)
  1. Graphic novels. [1. Graphic novels. 2. Basketball--Fiction.] I. Aburto, Jesus, ill. II. Esparza, Andres, ill. III. Maese, Fares, ill. IV. Title.
PZ7.7.C54Ho 2011
741.5'973--dc22   2010032813

My name's Trey McTiernan.

This is the biggest game of my life.

We're two points behind with only a few seconds remaining.

The ball's in my hands.

If we win, we head to the State Finals...

Meet Griffin Henshaw.

He's the former captain of the Goliaths...

...the team we have to beat in three weeks if we want a shot at State.

I'd forgotten how fast he was.

STEAL!

Heh.

WHOOSH!

Now watch this . . .

Beautiful putback by Griffin Henshaw!

SWISHH!

Griff *was* cocky...

Dude, get your head in the game. I can't do this by myself.

...but he had a point.

Come on, Trey! Snap out of it!

After that, I had no trouble focusing.

BBZZZZZZZZZZTT!!

Moments later, down by two points...

...I won the game with a buzzer-beater.

SWOOSH!

THE SPARTANS HAVE BEATEN THE TIGERS!!!

Psst, hey Trey!

Look who Griffin is talking to.

Hey, guys! Thanks for coming out!

Nice game, Griff!

His old teammates from the Goliaths!

Ready for next Saturday?

Ha! Are you?

I bet he's telling them our weak spots, how our plays work — everything.

Maybe he's just hanging out with his friends, Max . . .

Don't be stupid. He's a rat, and you know it.

What if Max was right?

Let's go grab some pizza.

SLAP!

Great idea!

I decided to find out for myself.

27

Nope.

I'm a Spartan now, so I'll eat like one.

None of the guys would ever try octopus — but I didn't tell *him* that!

I had to admit it: Griffin had guts ...

... even if *his* ended up all over the gym floor later that day.

BLECH*!!!*

I didn't know what to do.

CLICK

Coach! I didn't hear —

I overheard Max complaining about you not doing what he asked.

You know, trick Griff and

Before I knew it, the day of the big game arrived.

Welcome to the Spartans' arena . . .

. . . where no one gets out alive!

The game was intense, right from the start.

Everyone brought their best stuff.

FWIPPP!

From Will's lightning-fast passes...

...to Hugh's fadeaway jumper.

We were in sync.

Griffin's hot streak didn't last.

The Goliaths locked him down with double and triple teams.

They started sinking buckets and making defensive stops.

SWISH!

BANK

Before I knew it, we were behind.

03:37

GOLIATHS 52 · 2 · SPARTANS 44

I was starting to wonder about Griffin again.

Griff was wide open.

But I hesitated.

Now the Goliaths just have to run out the clock!

Not if we can help it!

Get him.

Give us your best game, Griff.

You got it.

That was it. That's what he promised his former teammates. His *friends*.

Steal*!!!*

Yeah!!!

Way to go, Spartans!

Sushi's on me, guys!

Like I said — Griffin's got guts.

SPARTANS RALLY TOGETHER TO OVERCOME GOLIATHS

THE MBERS

LEADERS:
TS: GRIFFIN, 33
STS: TREY, 11
KS: JAY, 4

STORY: The Spartans were convinced a rat was on their team — and that his name was Griffin Henshaw. But as the game against the Goliaths went on, the Spartans realized that Griff was on their side — he torched his former team for 33 points! Trey McTiernan said, "Once we saw how committed Griff was to playing his best against his friends, we knew he was a Spartan at heart."

SZ *POSTGAME EXTRA*

WHERE *YOU* ANALYZE THE GAME!

BLZ vs BKS
3-1
TGR vs ROR
33-32
EAG vs BAN
14-7
SPA vs WLD
4-3
BAN vs ROR
21-15
ROR vs LIG
4-3
BLZ vs BKS
3-1

Basketball fans got a real treat today when the Spartans faced off against the Goliaths. Let's go into the stands and ask some fans for their opinions on the day's big game ...

DISCUSSION QUESTION 1

Should trust be given or earned? Do you trust people right away, or does it take a while? Why?

DISCUSSION QUESTION 2

Who is your favorite Spartan? Griff, Trey, Max, Coach Schu? Why?

WRITING PROMPT 1

Are there any other ways that Trey could've found out whether or not Griffin could be trusted? Write down some methods for Trey to test Griff's loyalty.

WRITING PROMPT 2

Have you ever had to move to a new place? What do you think would be difficult about changing schools? Write about it.

GLOSSARY

ANTICIPATE   (an-TISS-i-pate)—to expect something to happen and be prepared for it

COCKY   (KOK-ee)—overconfident or too sure of oneself

FADEAWAY   (FAYD-uh-way)—a type of jump shot where the shooter fades backward while releasing the ball

FATE   (FATE)—what will happen

HESITATION   (hez-uh-TAY-shuhn)—pausing or waiting due to uncertainty

INTENSE   (in-TENSS)—very strong and unrelenting

RAT   (RAT)—a spy, or a disloyal and untrustworthy person

SUSHI   (SOO-shee)—a Japanese dish made of raw fish or seafood that is pressed into special rice

SUSPICIOUS   (suh-SPISH-uhss)—if you feel suspicious, you think that something seems wrong

SYNC   (SINK)—if you are in sync with someone, then you are working together perfectly with that person

EATORS

Scott Ciencin › Author

Scott Ciencin is a *New York Times* bestselling author of children's and adult fiction. He has written comic books, trading cards, video games, television shows, as well as many non-fiction projects. He lives in Sarasota, Florida with his beloved wife, Denise, and his best buddy, Bear, a golden retriever.

Aburtov › Managing Illustrator

Aburtov runs his own illustration studio called Graphikslava, where he manages many talented illustrators ...

Fernando Cano › Penciler

Fernando Cano is an emerging illustrator born in Mexico City, Mexico. He currently works as a full-time illustrator and colorist at Graphikslava studio. He has done illustration work for Marvel, DC Comics, and role-playing games like *Pathfinder* from Paizo Publishing. In his spare time, he enjoys hanging out with friends, singing, rowing, and drawing!

Andres Esparza › Inker

Andres Esparza has been a graphic designer, colorist, and illustrator for many different companies and agencies. Andres now works as a full-time artist for Graphikslava studio in Monterrey, Mexico. In his spare time, Andres loves to play basketball, hang out with family and friends, and listen to good music.

Fares Maese › Colorist

Fares Maese is a graphic designer and illustrator. He has worked as a colorist for Marvel Comics, and as a concept artist for the card and role-playing games *Pathfinder* and *Warhammer*. Fares loves spending time playing video games with his Graphikslava comrades, and he's an awesome drum player.

HOT SPORTS.
HOT
FORMAT!

GREAT CHARACTERS BATTLE FOR SPORTS GLORY IN TODAY'S HOTTEST FORMAT—GRAPHIC NOVELS!

ONLY FROM **STONE ARCH BOOKS**

Sports Illustrated KIDS
GRAPHIC NOVELS

THE FUN
DOESN'T STOP
HERE!

FIND MORE
GAMES
PUZZLES
CHARACTER!

www.capstonekids.com

Still want MORE? Find cool websites and more books like this one at www.Facthound.com. Just type in the Book 9781434222237 and you're ready to go!

AND FOR SPORTS HEADLINES, SCORES, SI KIDS.con
STATS, PHOTOS, COOL GAMES ...

STONE ARCH BOOKS

3 1901 05310 1608